For three city dwellers, Jamie, Jen, and Dora
—H.M.Z.

10 9 8 7 6 5 4 3 2 1
Text copyright © 2004 by Harriet Ziefert
Illustrations copyright © 2004 by Santiago Cohen
All rights reserved / CIP Data is available.
Published in the United States 2004 by
Blue Apple Books
515 Valley Street, Maplewood, N.J. 07040
www.blueapplebooks.com
Distributed in the U.S. by Chronicle Books
Printed in China
First Edition
ISBN 1-59354-064-7

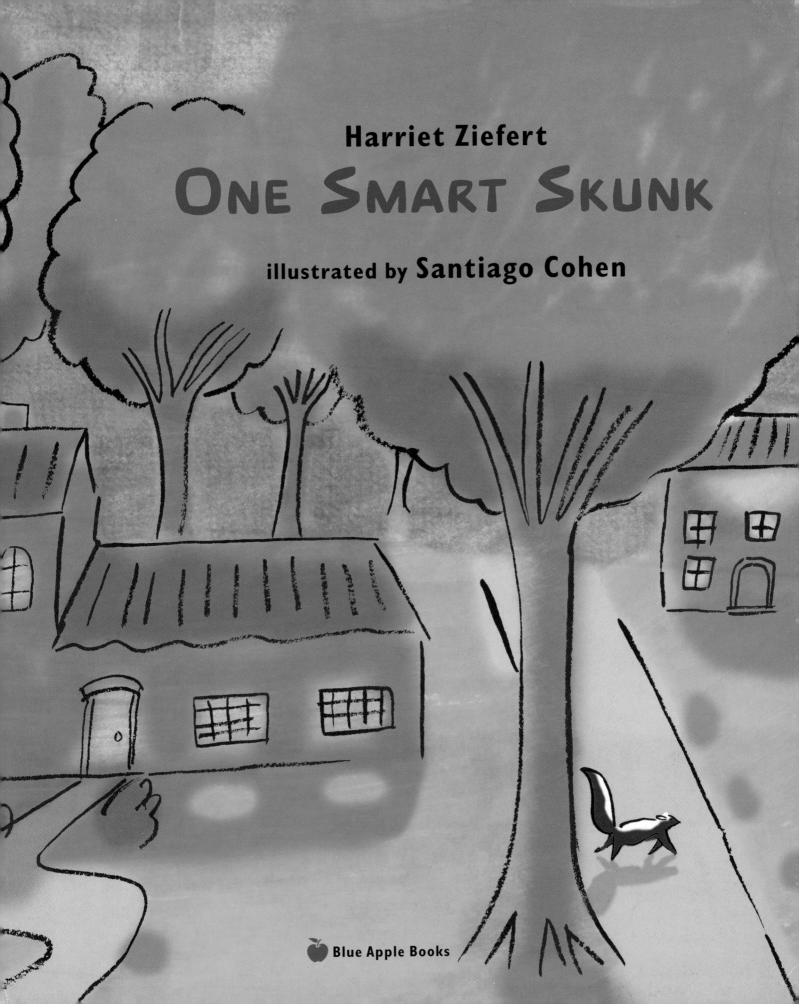

Harriet Ziefert

ONE SMART SKUNK

illustrated by **Santiago Cohen**

Blue Apple Books

Beamer smelled awful.
And it wasn't the first time.

"Beamer's been sprayed by a skunk!"
said Willy's mom.

"That dog will stink for days!"
said Willy's dad.

"Get away from me!" yelled Willy.
"And don't come back until you've
had a bath!"

Rebecca did not like being chased.

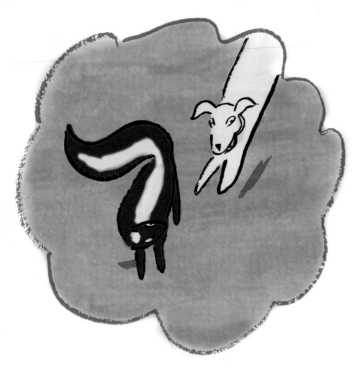

She did not like being interrupted
when she was trying to catch a mouse.

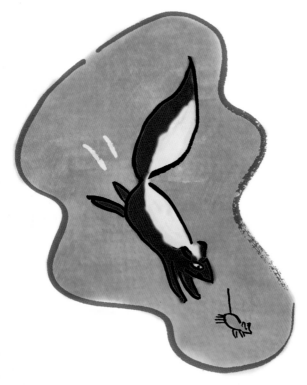

And she did not like to be surprised,
or pounced on, while she was eating.

One day, while Rebecca was digging for grubs,
she overheard an alarming conversation.

"I wouldn't be fooled by her sweet face,"
said a man's voice. "She's nothing but a tricky
little critter, and a smelly one at that!"

The voice continued.
"I think we should blast her!"

"OH NO!" cried a softer female voice.
"There is no need to hurt her.
If you don't bother her, she
won't bother you."

Rebecca relaxed. At least someone
knew she was harmless. But it was
a while before she dared to venture
out in the open.

Several days later Rebecca noticed
a metal-and-wire crate under the deck.
Somebody—probably the boy—had
worked hard on the decoration.

There was a small hooked rug,
a bed of straw, a pretty flower,
and a tiny dish of water. An odd-shaped
cracker with Cheddar cheese sat
on a napkin near the doorway.

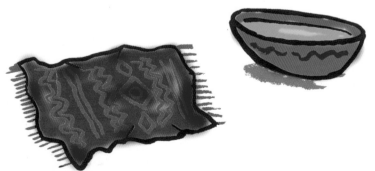

Rebecca approached the crate, her nose twitching.
The cheese smelled good, but she was suspicious.
She walked all around the wire house,
checking it out, but decided not to go inside.
She would wait.

The next day Rebecca watched Willy help his dad carry the wire house to the edge of their yard.

Willy's dad pulled open the door
and released two nervous squirrels,
who quickly ran up a tree.

Thank goodness Rebecca was smarter than the squirrels. If she hadn't been patient, she too might have fallen for the sweet smell of Cheddar cheese.

A few days later, Rebecca heard a familiar voice.
"It's time for us to have a heart-to-heart talk.
I've been watching you gather your things for a nest.
And you are definitely plumper around your middle.
One skunk is tolerable, but a family of skunks...impossible!"

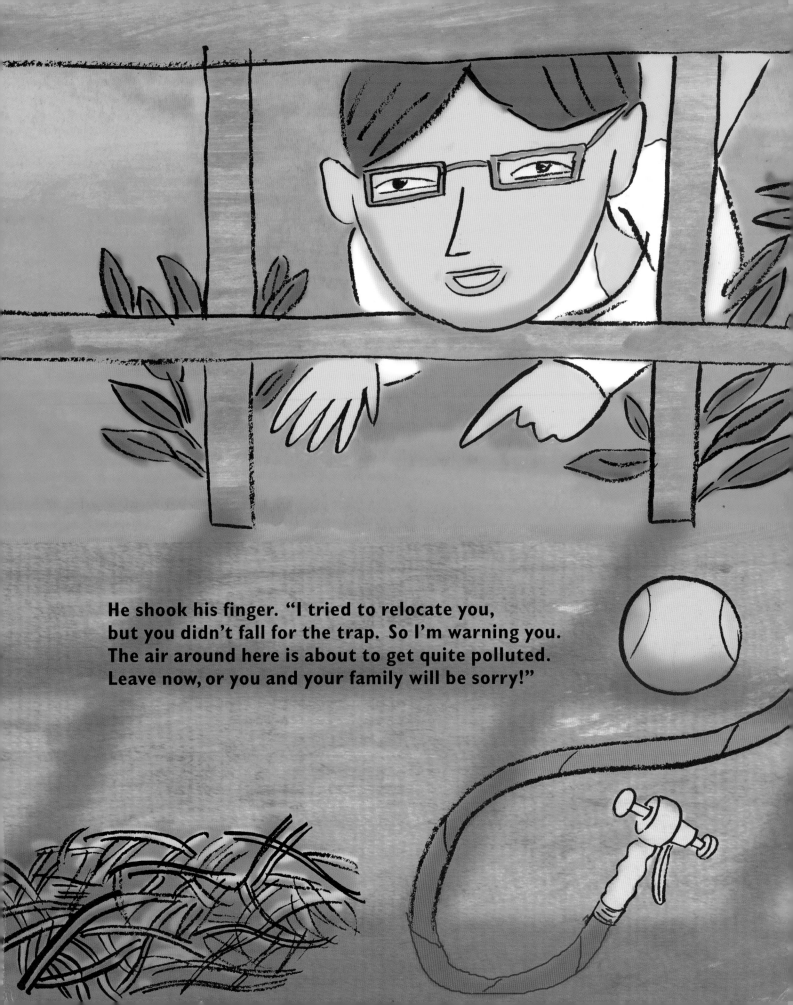

He shook his finger. "I tried to relocate you,
but you didn't fall for the trap. So I'm warning you.
The air around here is about to get quite polluted.
Leave now, or you and your family will be sorry!"

In the morning Willy's dad returned
with a large jar filled with small white balls.
Rebecca watched him from her hiding place.

He opened the jar and flung three big scoopfuls
of the stuff around the entrance to her nest.
He also threw a smelly rag on the ground.

Willy placed a boom box on
the deck above Rebecca's nest
and turned up the volume.

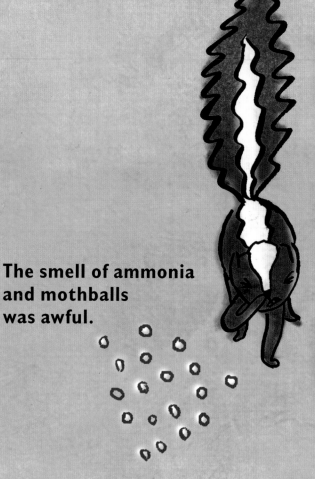

The smell of ammonia and mothballs was awful.

The sound of rap music was intolerable.

Rebecca got the message—this was no place to raise a family!

As soon as dusk came, Rebecca fled.

Rebecca left a note:

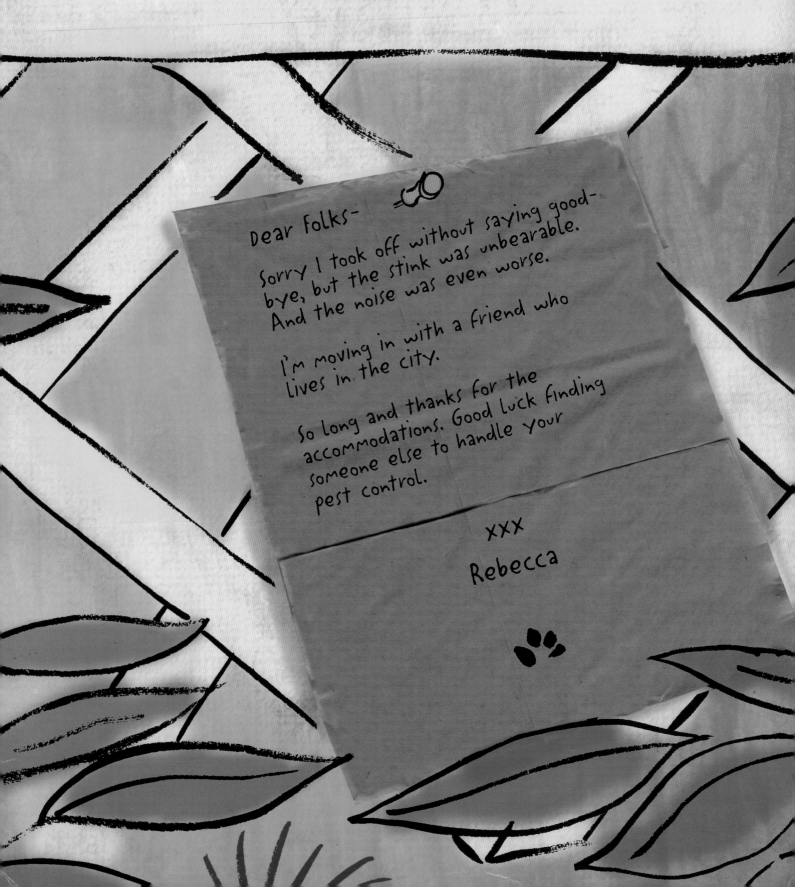

Rebecca traveled most of the night.
At daybreak she arrived in the city.

On her first evening in the city, Rebecca had
no problem finding her old friend. They climbed
a drainpipe together and watched the moon.
Rebecca had a good feeling about her new home.
She had no regrets.

Rebecca slept during the day. At night, she and her friend explored. No one bothered them as they walked up and down the avenues. The city was definitely a good place to raise a family!

Author's Note:

When an author stands in front of an audience of either children or grown-ups, he or she is bound to be asked: "How do you get your ideas?"

Book ideas come from many sources—a childhood experience, a photograph, a painting, a chance encounter in a playground, and in this instance, an article from a newspaper.

In August 1997 I read an article in the *New York Times* about the increase in the suburban skunk population. I thought it contained a lot of interesting information and clipped it for my files. Five years later, the smell of skunk in my backyard every morning for a week led me to reread the piece.

A few months later a drawing of a skunk by Santiago Cohen came across my desk. Once I had a skunk image in mind, I began to write. I decided to give the skunk a beautiful name, and she's been Rebecca since the first draft.

—HMZ

THE NE

For Maligned Skunks, The Ill Odor Is Lifting

In Suburbia, Their Numbers Are Rising While Their Reputation Is Improving

By JANE FRITSCH

STAMFORD, Conn.– There was a time, not long ago when a person could feel good about hating skunks. They were sneaky little varmints that dug up your lawn while you slept. And if you caught them at it, they didn't fight fair. . . .

"They are the most misunderstood animals around," said Laura Simon, a skunk rehabilitator from Bethany, Conn., who preaches greater compassion for the skunk.

"They're very fair little animals. They do a warning stamp with their front feet. Boom, boom, boom, boom. And they raise their tails. It's very fair."

And people are just beginning to realize the value of skunks, she said. They eat beetles, grubs and baby rats and mice, species that seem to have fewer human defenders. . . .

Ms. Simon who opens her Connecticut home to skunks in crisis, said humans have little to fear from the animals. She offered what is arguably the most useful and thought-provoking insight into skunks: They hate rap music.

"Can't stand it," she said.

Played at a high volume near a skunk's nest, rap music will induce a skunk to leave by nightfall, Ms. Simon said. "I guess the skunk says to itself, 'I can do better than this.' " . . .

Duke Ze

other rea
no other
how succ
together
a bit of N
of sports
Washing
"Rest
real ind
not an
talk sh
bert's
famou
and n

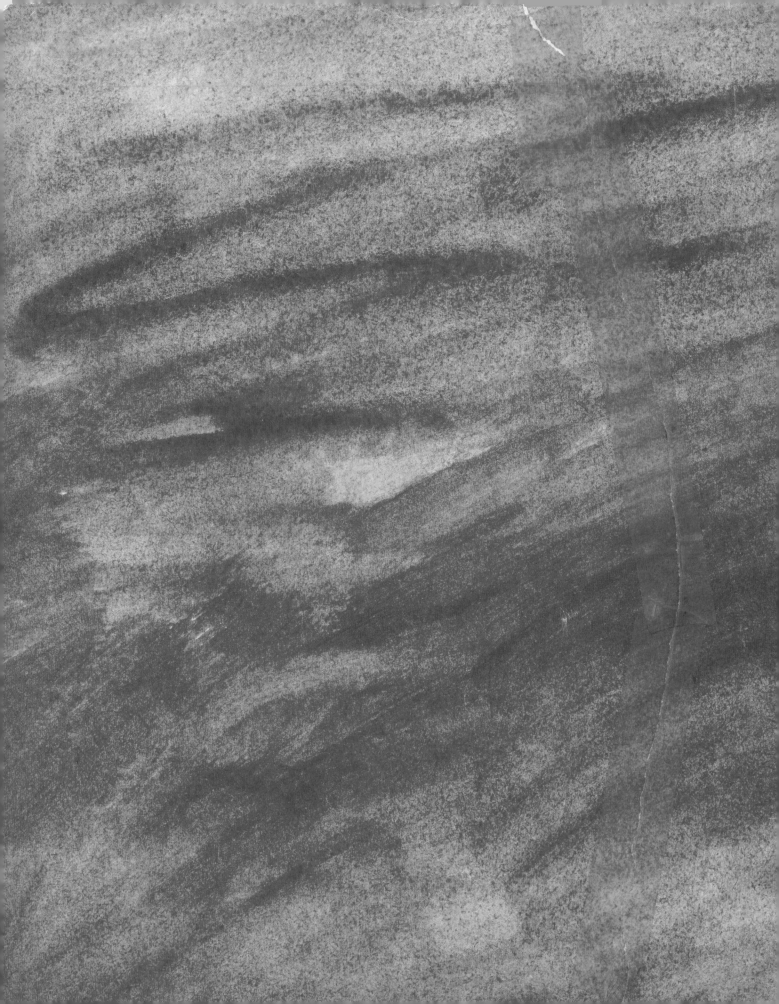